Windmill

Granny
Rabbit's cottage

Mr Mole:
Tradesmen's
entrance

This is the hill
they whizzed
down

They gathered
flowers here

Frankie
Frog's house

Mr Mole's
house

...da
...dmouse's
...age

Hedgehog's
house

BRIAN. H. KIDD
22/5/76

Tasseltip plays truant

Story by Sarah Cotton
Illustrations by
Ernest A. Aris and Roy Smith

*Based on the original characters
created by Dorothy Richards*

Publishers: Ladybird Books Ltd . Loughborough
© Ladybird Books Ltd 1975   *Printed in England*

TASSELTIP PLAYS TRUANT

"Hurry up, Tasseltip," called Mrs Rabbit, "or you will be late for school."

"I'm just coming," called back Tasseltip as he thumped noisily down the stairs.

"What a dreadful noise," said Mrs Rabbit. "Now, have you got everything?"

"Yes, I think so," replied Tasseltip, and he picked up his satchel after making sure the straps were properly fastened, then reached up to take his cap off the peg. Saying goodbye to his mother, he opened the door and went off whistling.

It was a lovely April morning. Little buds were beginning to appear on the trees, and here and there clumps of flowers were starting to grow.

"Today must be the first proper spring morning we have had this year," thought Tasseltip to himself. "It's far too nice a day to bother with having to go to school. I do wish it was a holiday."

Suddenly he thought, "Goodness, I'd better hurry, otherwise I am going to be late for school."

He started to run, because Mr Hare the schoolmaster was often very strict.

"Hurry up, slow coach," shouted Robert Rat, seeing his friend running towards him. "Isn't it a lovely day? Spring must be here at last."

They walked along together chattering loudly, not looking where they were going. Suddenly Tasseltip slipped on a wet stone and lost his balance. He tried waving his arms in the air to keep upright, but the strap on his satchel suddenly broke, and all his school books fell out in every direction. Poor Tasseltip sat down hurriedly with a bump and his books landed all about him.

Robert just stood there, laughing and laughing at his friend. "Ho ho, you have no idea how funny you looked. Waving your arms about and then sitting down so quickly. It was funny. Are you all right?" He helped Tasseltip to his feet.

"Yes, thanks," said Tasseltip, feeling a little foolish as he brushed his trousers. "No bones broken. I suppose I must have looked a bit silly," and he started to laugh as he gathered his books together.

"Bother, the strap has really broken — look," said Tasseltip, showing it to Robert. "I will just have to carry it like a bag instead of on my back."

"Come on, we'd better hurry or we will be late," said Robert. "I was late twice last week so I don't want to get into any more trouble. Mr Hare was very cross with me."

"I wish we didn't have to go to school," said Tasseltip, wistfully. "The winter has been so cold and seems to have gone on for such a long time, it's lovely to have a nice bright day like today. It does seem a pity to have to waste it by having to go indoors instead of stopping out here."

"Mmm. I agree with you," said Robert, looking towards the edge of the woods. "I'd like to spend my whole day fishing. I love going fishing."

"I don't think I have a favourite thing to do," said Tasseltip, wrinkling up his forehead as he spoke. "I like doing all sorts of things, so I don't really know which is the best. Oh, look Robert! Here comes old grumpy."

Mr Hedgehog was in a hurry and hardly bothered to glance at the two friends. He was carrying his spade and fork over his shoulder and was obviously going to spend the day working in the field. "You'd best be on your way or you'll be late for your lessons," he said as he passed them.

Tasseltip stepped after him quickly. "Mr Hedgehog," he called, "how would *you* like to go to school on a lovely spring morning like this? Wouldn't you much rather be out in the fresh air?"

"That's enough of your nonsense, Tasseltip Rabbit," said grumpy Mr Hedgehog. "I'm not answering your silly questions. I've had my days of learning and now it's your turn. Be off with you both, or you'll be really late," and Mr Hedgehog marched on, muttering under his breath.

"Well, I think Mr Hedgehog is pleased he doesn't have to go to school any more," said Tasseltip. "In fact, he probably didn't like it at all!"

"Do you think he was grumpy even when he was young?" said Robert thoughtfully. "I can't imagine him being young, can you?"

"Not really," said Tasseltip, giggling. Then he went on, "Robert, I've got an idea. Why don't we hide our books and go and play in the woods? Not bother about going to school today."

"But Tasseltip, we shall get into most terrible trouble," protested a thoroughly startled Robert.

"Look, there's a hole in the trunk of that tree," said Tasseltip, pointing to it. "Why not hide our books there until it's time to go home?"

It didn't take very long before Robert said, "All right, let's! What fun!" Then they both hid their satchels in the hollow tree.

After making quite sure their satchels and books were well and truly hidden, Tasseltip and Robert went off in the opposite direction to the school.

"Where are we going?" asked Robert.

"Nowhere in particular," said Tasseltip, hopping on one leg. "Let's just wait and see."

"Have you got your cap with you?" Robert suddenly asked his friend. "I want to watch you do your trick again."

Tasseltip stopped hopping about and took his cap out of his pocket. He put it on and then gave a toss of his head. Up flew the cap and as it started to fall, he stretched out his floppy left ear and caught it on the tip.

"My turn now," said Robert. "Watch me." He put his cap on his head and gave a tremendous toss. The cap sailed upwards and caught on a branch of a tree.

"Oh, bother!" said Robert, crossly.

Tasseltip laughed. "You did throw it a bit high. I'm not surprised it got caught on a tree. Let's see if we can find something long to knock it off."

"It's no use, we'll never reach it. I'll have to climb up," said Robert. Very slowly he began to climb the tree. Suddenly the branch he was holding on to broke and he fell right on top of Tasseltip. They both laughed as they scrambled to their feet.

"You two are going to be very late for school if you stand around like that," said a voice.

It was Friskie Squirrel and his sister!

"I'm so pleased to see you," said Robert, looking very relieved. "I was trying to do Tasseltip's trick with my cap, and you can see what has happened. Could you get it for me please, Friskie?"

"Of course I will," replied Friskie. "But this isn't your normal way to school, is it?"

"No," agreed Tasseltip, "but today is not normal. We have decided not to go to school, because it's the first day of spring."

"Oh! How exciting. I think it's a lovely idea," cried Susie enthusiastically. "We will join you." So saying she grabbed Friskie's bag and leapt up into the tree.

"Susie! Give me back my bag," said Friskie angrily. Then turning to Tasseltip he said, "Are you serious? You are not going to school?"

"We saw Mr Hedgehog earlier and he told us that his days of learning are over," said Tasseltip. "We can pretend ours are over, just for today."

"Well, it does sound fun," admitted Friskie, still very confused.

"Susie, will you get my cap for me, please?" called Robert. Susie carefully crawled along the branch and managed to reach the cap. Then she placed it on her head and crawled back safely to where the branch was stronger.

"I don't think it suits you, Susie," laughed Friskie. "Girls look better in hats!"

Susie made a face at Friskie and said, "I won't bring your bag down now. You'll have to come and get it," and she scampered down the tree trunk.

Robert reached out to take his cap when Susie suddenly tossed her head so that the cap flew off and she caught it very cleverly on her long, bushy tail.

"Susie!" called Friskie, climbing up the tree to get his satchel. "Give Robert back his cap at once."

"My sister seems to get worse and worse with all her tricks," said Friskie, once more down on the ground. "I think we had better go after her, or you will never get your cap, Robert."

So the three dashed along the path chasing naughty Susie, who still wore the cap on her tail. Eventually a rather breathless Tasseltip caught her and managed to take it away from her. "Here you are, Robert," he said.

"I say, what are you all doing here? You are going to be most frightfully late for school," said Frankie Frog, leaping towards them.

"Hello, Frankie, I'm glad we've seen you," said Tasseltip. "We are not going to school today, because it's the first day of spring. What I mean is, it will be much nicer to be out here than sitting in school."

"Goodness!" said Frankie. "What will Mr Hare say? When he sees all your empty places he *will* be cross." He put his hand in his pocket and brought out a green, mossy ball. "Look what I've got," and he held it out for the others to see.

"What fun! We can play with that," said Susie reaching out to take it from him.

"Hey, it's mine! I was only showing it to you, not giving it to you," protested Frankie. He clutched hold of it and started to run away from them.

"Come back, Frankie," shouted Tasseltip. "Susie wasn't really going to take it away from you."

It was no good. Frankie was almost out of sight. They all looked at each other in dismay.

"I don't think Frankie quite understood that we weren't going to go to school today," Tasseltip said. "I will see if I can catch him up."

Off went Tasseltip as fast as he could. When he was just behind Frankie, he reached out and caught him by the leg to stop him.

"I promise you that Susie won't take your ball away from you," he said, earnestly. "Pay attention, Frankie. We are not going to school today. It's my idea. It's because I think that spring is here at last. I tried to explain to you back there, but I don't think you were listening properly. Don't you think it will be much more fun to play outside instead of doing lessons?"

"Well, I don't know," said Frankie, rather doubtfully. He thought for a minute or two and then said, "All right, I will join you. But what are we going to do?"

"We'll find plenty to do!" replied Tasseltip, cheerfully. "Come on, let's go back to the others."

As they made their way back to where they had left the others, Frankie said, "It isn't very fair, Tasseltip, if we don't go to school. What about all the others? They might like to join us."

"Mmmm. You're quite right," agreed Tasseltip thoughtfully. "Come on, follow me!"

He crept towards the school with Frankie. The rest of the pupils were talking or playing games in the playground.

"Horace," whispered Tasseltip softly, "has Mr Hare arrived yet?"

Horace Hedgehog looked up. "Tasseltip! And Frankie! I was wondering where you were."

Tasseltip quickly explained. Then he said, "The thing is, Frankie thought it was only fair to come here and ask everybody whether they wanted a holiday as well, so here we are."

Horace stared in amazement then burst out laughing. "What a jolly idea," he chuckled. Then raising his voice, he said, "All those who would like a day off school follow Tasseltip. He will explain when we are out of sight of the school."

Tasseltip, Horace and Frankie raced off up the path followed by a little crowd of curious pupils.

"We wondered what you had been doing," said Robert to Tasseltip. "What a splendid idea to collect everybody."

Denis Duckling came up. "What's happening, Tasseltip?" he asked.

Once again Tasseltip explained to everyone how he felt like being outdoors on such a lovely day, how he thought it was the beginning of spring and how he wanted to share it with all his friends.

There was silence for a while, broken only by the odd bit of whispering, until large smiles began to appear on various faces as they got used to the idea. Soon all heads were nodding in agreement.

"Shall we go to Deep Wood then?" asked Tasseltip. "All those in favour, put up their hands."

All hands went up except that of little Freda Fieldmouse. She had caught her skirt on a spiky thorn, and was busy tugging at it to get it away. Suddenly she tugged extra hard and tore a large hole in it.

"Oh dear, what will my mother say?" wailed Freda, almost ready to burst into tears.

"Never mind that now, Freda," said Harriet Hare kindly. "We'll try to mend it later."

Little Felicity Dormouse stood watching clever Susie Squirrel turning cartwheel after cartwheel.

"Oh, you are so clever," she cried admiringly. "I do so wish I could learn to do that," and she clapped her hands together, not noticing that she had dropped her book on to the ground.

"Susie, stop showing off," said Tasseltip. "As no one seems to want to go to school, I suggest that we make our way to Deep Wood as quickly as possible. It would be silly if we were to be caught so near school."

"Tasseltip is quite right," confirmed Friskie. "Come on, everyone, all those of you who have got books or satchels should hide them carefully. You don't want to have to spend the whole day carrying them around with you."

Horace cleared some of the tall grass from around the bottom of a tree and carefully placed his slate with all the books and bags in a neat pile. Then he covered them up with grass so that they were completely hidden. Only Susie kept hers.

"Now, is everyone ready?" said Tasseltip, a bit impatiently. "If so, I think we must make a move. Follow me, all of you."

Denis Duckling was really enjoying himself. He and his brother David waddled as fast as they could behind Tasseltip, singing loudly.

"Oh look!" shouted Frankie Frog suddenly. "We've come as far as the old stream. Come on, let's all stay here for a while. We can play and paddle!"

"Hooray," shouted everyone, and they all sat down, pushing and jostling each other for the best places nearest the water's edge.

"Ooh! It's cold," said Denis, waving his feet in the air to dry them after paddling in the water.

"Sssh," said Frankie, sitting up hurriedly. "I hear something."

They all listened, and to their amazement a head popped out of a hole half way up the trunk of the tree opposite them. It was a very wide awake, cross-looking, Mr Owl. He glared down at them and said, "What are you all doing here? Why aren't you at school? How dare you make a noise when I am trying to have a rest?" His head disappeared, then popped out again for a moment as he said, "Be off with you immediately and don't come back again!"

"Perhaps we had better go straight on towards Deep Wood," said Tasseltip to Friskie.

"Wait a minute," said Horace Hedgehog. "Tasseltip, I think we've lost Freda Fieldmouse. Perhaps she was frightened by old Owl."

"Bother. I'll see if I can find her," said Tasseltip. "I forgot that Mr Owl always terrifies her."

"We'll help," said the Squirrels.

"I will, too," called out Frankie.

So the Squirrels went back the way they had come, Frankie searched carefully along the stream, and Tasseltip walked away from the stream, up the grassy bank towards some large, overhanging bushes. He came across little Freda almost by accident as he nearly trod on her. She was crouched under a bush, crying quietly.

"Freda, stop being so silly," said Tasseltip, helping her to get up. "Old Owl is fast asleep. He's certainly not going to bother about you. Do stop crying and come and join the others. Frankie says we can play with his new ball. Cheer up."

So poor little Freda sniffed hard and dried her tears. Holding onto Tasseltip's paw very tightly, she walked back with him to where they had left the others.

"I've found her," called Tasseltip. "Somebody go and tell the Squirrels and Frankie the search is over." Horace Hedgehog went off to get them.

"I think we are far enough away from Owl if we play here for a while," said Tasseltip.

"If we divide ourselves into two teams," said Friskie, "then we can all play with the ball."

"Good idea," said Tasseltip and he felt in his pocket and found a penny. "Shall we toss to see who shall choose a team first?"

Friskie won and soon they were all divided up. Frankie Frog had found a large stick to use as a bat and he was soon in position to start the game.

"Are you all in your places?" asked Tasseltip, looking around. "Let's start now."

He ran a few paces and then tossed the ball at Frankie, who swung his bat back and hit the ball in the direction of Robert Rat. Robert missed it.

Tasseltip bowled again and again until at last Frankie made a mistake. He hit the ball right into the middle of the stream.

"Sorry, I didn't mean to do that!" said Frankie.

"Come over here," called Tasseltip, peering into the water. "Can you reach it, Frankie?"

Frankie went to the edge of the stream and peered into the water. Getting down on his knees he pushed up his sleeve and grabbed hold of what he thought was the ball. As he brought it out of the water, everybody started to laugh.

The ball had begun to fall to pieces in the water and was now just a handful of soggy green strands of moss and grass!

"I am very sorry, everyone," said Frankie, "but I think that's the end of our ball game."

"Never mind, I've got an idea," said Tasseltip. "Let's go over to those trees." He started to pull long strands of ivy off the trees.

"I thought that if we could bind them together somehow we could make a swing," he said.

"Sounds a splendid idea," said Friskie. "Why don't we try plaiting them together? You need three strands at a time."

"Right," agreed Tasseltip. So they busied themselves plaiting together the long strands of ivy whilst Robert and Frankie organised the others to play leap frog.

In no time at all the ropes were ready.

"Susie," called Friskie, "I'm going to need your help," and he quickly explained what he wanted her to do. In a matter of moments they were both sitting in the tree tying the rope on to the strongest-looking branches.

"I say, this is going to be fun," said Horace to Frankie Frog.

"Well, I can see one problem," replied Frankie.

"Oh? What's that?" asked Horace.

"Well, how are we going to sit on it?" said Frankie. "We will need a seat."

"That's easy," said Jeremy Thrush who had been listening. "Why not use a flat piece of wood?"

"If we can find one," said Frankie.

Susie was feeling a bit mischievous. "Frankie, what about using this?" she called. As Frankie came over to the tree and looked up, Susie threw down her heavy satchel. Frankie was so surprised, it landed right on his toe!

"Owwwwww!" shrieked Frankie. "You did that on purpose. Just you wait!" He clutched hold of his sore foot, hopping up and down on one leg.

"I thought it might come in useful if I kept it with me," thought Susie, climbing down the tree. All the friends were gathered around Frankie who was still hopping about, making an awful fuss. Picking up the satchel, Susie carefully tied it on to the rope, then sat down on it to test it. Pushing off with her toes, she was soon swinging happily.

"Look at Susie!" cried Felicity. "Oh, that does look fun."

"Well done, Susie, it was a clever idea of yours to use your satchel as a seat," said Tasseltip. "Now, who's to be first? Come on, Freda, it will be quite safe. Susie has tested it."

"You won't make me go very high, will you?" gasped Freda, as Robert started to push her.

At first she seemed to be thoroughly enjoying herself, until Robert forgot. He gave a tremendous push and the swing went so high that Freda thought she would go higher than the trees.

"Stop! Stop!" she shrieked. "Help, stop!"

"Hold on, Freda," shouted Tasseltip. "We'll soon have you down. Just hold on, you'll be quite safe."

At last a very frightened Freda Fieldmouse tumbled on to the ground.

"What was the matter?" asked Tasseltip. "Didn't you enjoy it?"

"Oh yes, at first it was very exciting, and then I suddenly went so high," said Freda, sniffing.

"Silly thing," said Tasseltip. "Cheer up. Are you

all right now?'' Freda nodded, smiling tearfully.

Soon she was forgotten as the others took turns to have a swing. Denis and David Duckling sat on the swing together and had a marvellous time.

"There's a lovely view of all the tree tops,'' squawked Denis. "It's just like flying.''

"Now it's my turn,'' said Frankie Frog. "I won't need any one to push me, Tasseltip. I can do it on my own.''

So he sat down on the seat and pushed the ground away with his feet. Soon he was up in the air, getting higher and higher.

"Be careful,'' called Tasseltip.

"I'm perfectly all right,'' answered Frankie, as he went higher and higher.

"Look! He's going to touch the top of the tree,'' whispered an astonished Harriet Hare. "Oh look! Look at the branch!'' and she pointed to one of the branches the swing was tied to.

Very slowly it was giving way!

"Stop at once, Frankie,'' called Tasseltip urgently. "Stop at once, the branch is beginning to break. You'll fall.''

"I can't stop in time," shouted Frankie in alarm. "Oh goodness, I'll have to jump. Out of the way, everyone!" and he leapt off the swing and splashed into the stream.

"We'll have to find something else to play with," said Tasseltip to Friskie and Robert as Frankie climbed out of the stream, dripping. "The swing is useless." He handed Susie's satchel to her.

Then he carefully wound the strands of ivy around the tree. "Just in case someone tries to swing on it," he said to Robert.

Frankie joined them, jumping up and down to dry his clothes.

"Perhaps you ought to go home," said Susie. "You look awfully wet. Doesn't it make you feel miserable?"

"I don't mind," said Frankie. "I've wrung the water out of my coat and the sun will soon dry everything. I'm used to being wet. I don't think I have ever seen you get wet, have I?"

"No, I hate it," admitted Susie. "When it rains I stay at home nice and snug."

"Come on, everybody," said Tasseltip. "Let's keep heading towards Deep Wood."

43

Tasseltip led the way and they soon left behind the bubbling stream and were walking through the spinney and out into the meadow.

"I thought we could go through Hedgerow Corner and then into Deep Wood," said Tasseltip to Friskie.

"All right," said Friskie. "But you never know what else we might find to do before we ever get to Deep Wood."

"You are quite correct, Friskie Squirrel," said a stern voice loudly. "Now you have all found something else to do!"

No one had noticed the tall figure of Mr Hare until he spoke to Friskie.

"I hope one of you will be kind enough to explain your behaviour. What is the meaning of all this? Why are you not sitting at your desks in the classroom? Frankie Frog, you are soaking wet. Now, hurry up! I want an explanation immediately!" and Mr Hare waved his cane at them.

"Well," said Tasseltip, "please, sir . . .," but he got no further, for there was suddenly a piercing scream.

Mr Hare told them to stay where they were, and hurried off in the direction of the scream. It was little Freda Fieldmouse, hanging from a bush.

The moment she had seen the schoolmaster she had been so frightened that she had run away to hide. When she was crawling under a bush to hide, somehow her skirt had got caught on one of the branches and she had been lifted into the air and was now unable to move.

After Mr Hare had unhooked Freda, he strode quickly back to his other pupils and, placing himself in front of the tree, he faced Tasseltip.

"Silence, everybody," he said sternly. "Now, Tasseltip Rabbit, just why are you and the rest of your friends playing truant?"

Tasseltip shuffled towards Mr Hare, feeling rather miserable. Hanging his head, he said in a very quiet voice, "Please, sir, it was all my fault. You see, it was such a lovely morning, I thought that spring must be here at last. Everywhere you look there are buds and flowers starting to grow. Well, it was because of that I persuaded everyone to stay away. I thought we could look at all the new things." Tasseltip stared at the ground.

"I see," said Mr Hare, looking slowly at all the different faces that were staring anxiously back at him. "I am surprised at you all," he said, shaking his head. "Tell me, Tasseltip, what had you planned to do for the rest of the day? What were you going to do at lunch time?"

Tasseltip looked up at Mr Hare. "Please, sir, I didn't really think as far ahead as lunch time."

"I see," said Mr Hare again. "There is one more question I would like to ask you, Tasseltip Rabbit, since this playing truant seems to be your idea. Do you plan to play truant every sunny day?"

Tasseltip was feeling very unhappy. He couldn't understand what had made him behave so badly.

"Please, sir," said Tasseltip, "I can't explain very clearly, but somehow today did seem rather special. I don't think there will be another like it."

"I am glad to hear it, Tasseltip Rabbit," said Mr Hare in his sternest voice. "I have decided, as this is the first time, not to punish any of you. However, if I ever catch any one of you trying to play truant again, well . . . I shall punish the culprit most severely. I hope that is understood?"

"Oh, yes, sir," chorused his pupils.

"Tasseltip, go with Robert and Friskie and bring me that log from over there," said Mr Hare, pointing to a fallen log.

When they had brought it to him, he sat down stiffly and said, "Gather round, all of you. Now, as you all appear to be so interested in nature study, I have decided we shall spend the rest of the morning out here having a lesson."

Everyone smiled with relief and sat down.

"How many of you have got your books with you?" asked Mr Hare, and only Susie Squirrel was able to put up her hand.

"Very well," said Mr Hare, "we will continue with the lesson and then you may all collect your books and satchels from wherever you have left them as you return to school. Is that understood?"

Everyone chorused, "Yes," and then fell silent as Mr Hare began the lesson.

"Gosh, we were lucky he was in a good mood," whispered Tasseltip to Friskie.

"Tasseltip Rabbit!" said Mr Hare suddenly. "I hope it is not you I can hear whispering?"

"Oh, no, sir!" said Tasseltip and he immediately began to concentrate on the lesson.

The Squirrels lived in these woods

Mr Mole: Tradesmen's entrance

This is the hill they whizzed down

The flower show was held in the Deep Wood

They gathered flowers here

WEASEL HOUSE

Mr Mole's house

They looked for the 'Boozle' here

Hedgehog's house

The Voles lived in this old stump